Yuki's Ride Home

Manya Tessler

BLOOMSBURY
CHILDREN'S
BOOKS

Special thanks to Ronnie Ann Herman, Haruka Hyuga and her family, and, of course, my beloved Roumen

---

Typeset in Chianti
Art created with pencil sketches, patterned paper, and digital techniques
Book design by Nicole Gastonguay

Published by Bloomsbury U.S.A. Children's Books
175 Fifth Avenue, New York, NY 10010
Distributed to the trade by Holtzbrinck Publishers

Library of Congress Cataloging-in-Publication Data
Tessler, Manya.
Yuki's ride home / by Manya Tessler.—1st U.S. ed.
p.   cm.
Summary: After an enjoyable day at her grandmother's house,
Yuki tries to gather all her courage to ride her bicycle home in the evening fog.
ISBN-13: 978-1-59990-023-0 • ISBN-10: 1-59990-023-8 (hardcover)
ISBN-13: 978-1-59990-163-3 • ISBN-10: 1-59990-163-3 (reinforced bdg.)
[1. Grandmothers—Fiction. 2. Courage—Fiction. 3. Bicycles and bicycling—Fiction. 4. Fear of the dark—Fiction.] I. Title.
PZ7.T284Yu 2008   [E]—dc22   2007025066

First U.S. Edition 2008
Printed in Malaysia
1 3 5 7 9 10 8 6 4 2 (hardcover)
1 3 5 7 9 10 8 6 4 2 (reinforced)

All papers used by Bloomsbury U.S.A. are natural, recyclable products
made from wood grown in well-managed forests. The manufacturing processes
conform to the environmental regulations of the country of origin.

With love to Nanny and Grandma

Yuki kissed her mom good-bye and
pedaled over the bridge to Grandma's.
She couldn't wait to tell Grandma her news.

"Grandma! Grandma!" called Yuki. "I'm going to ride home all by myself today."

Grandma's dog, Biscuit, ran over and licked Yuki on the cheek.

"Does your mom know about this?" asked Grandma.

"Sure. She said that I'm big enough now."

"That's true. Pretty soon you'll be taller than me." Grandma laughed.

"Come on, Grandma," said Yuki,
"let's go feed the koi."

"Good morning," said Yuki to the koi
as she tossed them some turnip leaves.

Grandma's cat, Milk,
dipped her paw in the water.

"I think she wants to play with the koi," said Yuki, laughing.

Grandma brought out a snack of
sweet bean buns. Yuki fed her crumbs to
the seagulls that visited Grandma's yard.
"How could I forget you?" chuckled
Yuki as she handed Grandma's bird,
Ribbon, a little piece.

Hot from the midday sun, Grandma
and Yuki sat in the shade on Grandma's
back porch and made origami animals.

For dinner, Grandma made her special udon noodle soup—it was Yuki's favorite. Yuki felt the warm steam on her face as she slurped the chunky noodles.

After dinner, they picked the perfect spot to snuggle while the sun set. Yuki leaned her head on Grandma's shoulder.

"You know," said Grandma, "when your mom was your age, we would come down here and listen to the night music."

Yuki closed her eyes and listened.

The trees rustled.

The waves lapped at the shore.

And a fish splashed in the water, sprinkling Yuki and Grandma.

Yuki opened her eyes to see the fish, but she was surprised to find that the fog had rolled in.

"Mom will worry if I'm not home soon," thought Yuki.

As Grandma and Yuki walked back to the house, Grandma held Yuki's hand. It felt cold.

"Why don't I walk you home?" Grandma offered.

"I'll be okay," Yuki said.

Yuki said good-bye and sat down on her bike.
"I can hardly see anything," thought Yuki.

The path snaked down the hill into a mouth of mist.
Ka-tung ka-tung beat Yuki's heart.

Then Grandma had an idea.

"Wouldn't you like some company?" she asked. "Biscuit, Milk, and Ribbon would love a ride on your bike. Maybe they could have a sleepover at your house."

"Thanks, Grandma!" said Yuki. "I'll take good care of them."

Yuki began pedaling through the mist. Her knees rose and fell in time to Ribbon's cheerful song. Milk's soft, fuzzy tail tickled Yuki's hand, and Biscuit covered Yuki's neck in warm, wet kisses.

"When I get home," explained Yuki, "my mom will tuck me into my warm bed. She'll sing me a lullaby, and then she'll kiss me good night."

But then Yuki thought about Grandma,
alone in her house.

Yuki turned to Biscuit. "Who will keep
Grandma company tonight?"

Yuki stopped her bike and helped everyone down.

"What will she do without your good-night kisses, Biscuit? Milk, without you, who will keep Grandma warm? And Ribbon, Grandma loves your lullabies. I think you should all go home to Grandma."

Yuki watched as Grandma's little family of pets followed the path back home.

The bridge to Yuki's house rose up like a wall. Yuki's stomach flipped, and she sat still on her bike.

Yuki heard the gentle *slish-slosh* of the water, the
gulp-gulp of a frog, and the *trill-trill* of the crickets.
The night music was all around her.

Yuki relaxed. She stood up tall and pushed down
hard on the pedals. The bridge was slippery and
steep, but Yuki kept pedaling.

With one final push, Yuki sailed over the bridge . . . past the
night shadows . . . up the path to her home . . . and into her
mother's arms.

"How was your big ride home?" asked
Yuki's mom.
"I have so much to tell you," said Yuki.

Cozy under the covers, Yuki listened to the sounds of the night. She thought about her ride home, and about her grandma, just across the bridge, snuggled up in bed with her pets.